anything

cloverleaf books™

Off to School

Tanya Takes the School Bus

by **Martha E. H. Rustad**

Illustrated by **Paula J. Becker**

M MILLBROOK PRESS • MINNEAPOLIS

For Maya—MEHR

Millbrook Press
A division of Lerner Publishing Group, Inc.
241 First Avenue North
Minneapolis, MN 55401 USA

For reading levels and more information, look up this title at
www.lernerbooks.com.

Main body text set in Slappy Inline 22/28.
Typeface provided by T26.

Library of Congress Cataloging-in-Publication Data

The Cataloging-in-Publication Data for *Tanya Takes the
School Bus* is on file at the Library of Congress.
ISBN 978-1-5124-3939-7 (lib. bdg.)
ISBN 978-1-5124-5580-9 (pbk.)
ISBN 978-1-5124-5108-5 (EB pdf)

Manufactured in the United States of America
1-42152-25425-12/16/2016

TABLE OF CONTENTS

Chapter One

Back to School

I get to ride the bus to school this year! I'm excited and a little nervous.

Welcome back to school!

Lunch Cards

I met my bus driver, Anne. She taught me how to be safe near the bus.

Bus Safety

I learned that if I cannot see the driver, she cannot see me.

A crossing arm on the front of a bus shows how far to stay from the front of the bus.

Chapter Two

The Bus Stop

On the first day of school, Dad and I go to the bus stop a little early. I don't want to miss the bus!

We stay off the street and away from traffic. That way, we'll stay safe while we wait for the bus.

When the bus comes, we step back from the curb and wait for it to stop. **The lights flash red.**

I know flashing lights mean that cars behind the bus must stop. Anne the bus driver taught us that!

The lights on a bus may flash yellow or red. Yellow lights tell traffic to slow down. Red lights and a stop sign on the side of the bus tell other cars to stop.

Anne opens the door. "Good morning," she says. "All aboard!"

We get on the bus one at a time. I hold the
railing and walk up the steps.

Chapter Three

On the Bus

I hear my friend Zoe call my name.
She saved me a seat on the bus.

We talk quietly so we don't bother the bus driver.

It is a good idea to keep the bus aisles clear so no one gets hurt.

At the next stop, Marco gets on. Anne uses the lift door to help him get on the bus.
I wave at Marco to say hello.

Soon we are at school. We stay in our seats until the bus stops.

"Here we are!" says Anne.
"Have a great day at school!"

Chapter Four
A Safe Ride Home

The school day is done. We line up outside, and a teacher checks to make sure we get on the right buses.

I can see my dad waiting for me at the bus stop when we get to my neighborhood. **Today was a great day!** I can't wait to ride the bus tomorrow.

Alphabet Bus Game

Bus riders use quiet voices so they do not bother the bus driver. Here is a quiet game you can play on the bus.

1) Invite a friend or two to play.
   The person whose birthday is next goes first.

2) The first player looks for the letter *A*. Look on road signs and billboards.

3) When an *A* is found, the next player looks for the letter *B*.

4) Keep on going through the whole alphabet. See how far you can get before it's time to get off the bus!

Tip: Some letters might be hard to find. Work as a team to find tricky letters such as *Q* and *X*.

GLOSSARY

aisle: a narrow place to walk between rows of seats on a bus

bus stop: a place where a bus driver picks up passengers

curb: the edge of a sidewalk by the street

lift door: a door with a built-in elevator. Bus drivers use lift doors to help passengers in wheelchairs board the bus.

traffic: cars, buses, and trucks driving on a road

BOOKS

Bloom, Paul. *The School Rules: Rules on the Bus.* New York: Gareth Stevens, 2015. Learn the rules to follow when you are riding a bus.

Jennings, Rosemary. *Safe on the School Bus.* New York: PowerKids, 2017. Read more about safety on the school bus.

Morey, Allan. *School Buses.* Minneapolis: Bullfrog Books, 2015. Find out about the parts of a school bus.

WEBSITES

Facts about Buses
http://www.scienceforkidsclub.com/buses.html
Learn about the history of the school bus and why buses are yellow.

Kids, the School Bus, and You
http://www.nhtsa.gov/people/injury/buses/kidsschoolbus_en.html
See more bus safety facts for kids and parents.

LERNER *e* SOURCE™

Expand learning beyond the printed book. Download free, complementary educational resources for this book from our website, www.lernerresource.com.